Smart ABOUT Safety

Fire Prevention

by **Teddy Slater**   illustrated by **Anthony Lewis**

Scholastic Inc.
New York   Toronto   London   Auckland
Sydney   Mexico City   New Delhi   Hong Kong

For Gina Shaw, who makes it all so easy.
— T.S.

ISBN 978-0-545-24603-3

Text copyright © 2010 by Teddy Slater
Illustrations copyright © 2010 by Anthony Lewis

All rights reserved. Published by Scholastic Inc.

SCHOLASTIC, SMART ABOUT SAFETY, and associated logos
are trademarks and/or registered trademarks of Scholastic Inc.

12 11 10 9 8 7 6 5 4 3 2 1   10 11 12 13 14 15/0

Printed in the U.S.A.   40

First printing, September 2010

Sara made her brother Sam a chocolate cake for
his birthday. But it wasn't exactly a chocolate cake.
It was a chocolate *mud* cake.

"That doesn't look like a real cake," Sam said.

"It's not finished yet," Sara said.

She stuck nine candles into her cake.

Then she picked up some matches and tried to light one.

"Hey!" Sam shouted. "Don't you know how dangerous it is to use matches?"

"I was just going to light a small flame for the candles," Sara said.

"Even a small flame can become a big fire," Sam said.

"Just listen to what happened to Bubba."

"Who's Bubba?" Sara asked.

"Bubba was a bear who lived in the woods," Sam began. "Bubba's big brother warned him never to play with matches. The woods were full of trees that could easily go up in flames.

"One day, Bubba's family went off to pick berries.

Bubba had a tummy ache, so he stayed back.

His mother wrapped him up in a fuzzy blanket.

'Stay here and rest,' she said. 'We'll be home soon.'

"Bubba tried to rest, but he was too cold.

He decided to make a small fire.

Bubba placed a few sticks inside a circle of stones.

That's the way his father always did it.

"Bubba lit a match very carefully and threw it onto the sticks.

He knew he wasn't supposed to play with matches.

But this wasn't playing.

He needed the fire to keep warm.

"Bubba curled up near his fire. Not too near, though.

He didn't want his blanket to catch fire.

Now Bubba felt warm and cozy.

"Suddenly, a cold wind shook the trees.

The leaves fluttered.

The fire sputtered.

A dry leaf fell from a tree and burst into flames.

"The burning leaf blew through the woods.

More leaves began to burn.

A stick caught fire, and then another.

Soon the forest was thick with smoke.

"Bubba's family raced home.

They picked up Bubba and ran away from the fire.

The bears were all safe," Sam said. "But the fire burned

lots of trees before a big rain finally put it out."

"Oh, no!" Sara said.

"Oh, yes," Sam said. "When it comes to fire, you must be very careful."

SAFETY TIPS

Never light a match by yourself.

Ask a grown-up for help
if you want to cook in the kitchen.

Always keep your distance
from a burning stove top, candle,
or bonfire — especially if you're
wearing loose clothing.